D1143302

MY LITTLE ANIMAL FRIENDS AT NIGHT-TIME

Gerda Muller

TREASURE PRESS

French text for *Dodo, The Little Hamster*
and *Little Owl* by Résie Pouyanne
French text for *Chippy, The Racoon* by Marie Tenaille
English translation by Angela Wilkes

First published in Great Britain in 1986 by
Treasure Press
59 Grosvenor Street
London W1

Reprinted 1988

Illustrations copyright © Gautier-Langereau 1981
English text copyright © Octopus Books 1986

ISBN 1 85051 117 9

Printed in Czechoslovakia
50612/2

Dodo,
the Little Hamster

Dodo is a young golden hamster which
Christine has given to Mary and Bruno.
Christine's hamsters are grey, brown,
cream and even pale pink. But Mary and
Bruno have chosen Dodo, the prettiest
one of them all, and have taken him
home with them.

He sits on the table and puts his paws together.
'Are you hungry? Have a carrot.'
Dodo takes it and has a nibble, but he doesn't
swallow anything.

Hamsters store their food in
their pouches. Look at Dodo.

Dodo's face becomes fatter
and fatter on one side,
but he holds up his paws
for Mary to feed him.

Dodo stuffs the whole crust
into his other pouch.

In this way
a hamster fills his pouches
full of provisions.

Bruno puts Dodo back into his cosy, warm box.
'Night, night, Dodo!'
But like all mice Dodo is especially wide
awake . . . at night-time.
When everything is quiet
this is how Dodo spends his time:

First, he empties out his food, wiping his paws
across his pouches, and he puts it in a
pile in the corner. Then he gnaws through the
cardboard box and wriggles out of his prison.
He finds the parents' newspapers and shreds

them into thousands of tiny pieces which
he carries back to his box. Dodo makes at
least fifty trips, his pouches puffed out
with bits of paper so that he can make
them into a cosy nest.

14

Then he races up and down the curtains,
running as fast as he can ... Now he
feels hungry and hurries back to his
food, which he munches quietly.

Tired by so much activity,
he stops for a quick wash.

Having rubbed his ears and nose clean
Dodo wanders off to explore the
delights of the fruit basket. What a
tasty apple! And so the hectic night-
time play comes to an end and Dodo
curls up in a little ball to sleep.

16

In the morning Bruno picks up Dodo by the scruff
of his neck, one very sleepy and relaxed hamster.
'Ah, look!' says Mary. 'Dodo has begun to make a
nest. You know, Mum, it's wonderful having
Dodo. He can sleep while we are at school and
then wake up to play with us in the evening.'

'Yes,' says Mother, 'and he will nibble everything in the dark! When you get back from school you must go and find Mamie's old birdcage. Dodo can go in there at night and then we can sleep in peace.'

That evening, before dinner, Bruno and Mary ran up to the attic. Soon after they come down with Dodo's new house. They carefully sprinkle a layer of sand on the floor of the cage and place a small wooden box inside for Dodo's nest.

Bruno puts the dozing hamster in the cage, then he and Mary run off to put on their pyjamas, anxious to spend as much time as possible with Dodo before going to bed.

Dodo wakes up and his whiskers quiver.
He climbs up the bars of the cage and
tugs at them. He trots round the cage
and rubs himself against all the bars,
as if to say: 'This is my house! It belongs
to me. Leave it alone!'

The children give him some cotton wool and
a newspaper. He tears them up, chews them,
rolls them up and unrolls them and makes
his nest in the little box.
'Isn't he sweet!' cries Mary. 'Let's teach
him his name.' Bruno lifts Dodo out of the cage.

Mary holds up some grapes.
'Dodo,' she says, offering him a grape.
Dodo takes the grape and eats it. Mary
strokes his soft fur and he looks up
expectantly.
'Another grape Dodo?' Dodo is greedy
and eats the grapes straight away. It
doesn't take him long to learn his name.

Dodo intends to play now and he scampers up on
to Bruno's wrist. But look, he's wriggled up
Bruno's pyjama sleeve!

'Help, he's tickling me! He's
scratching me, help! Come out of there!'
Mary bursts out laughing. Bruno sits
perfectly still, watching his sleeve
bulge.

All of a sudden Dodo appears at Bruno's neck.
Sitting on his shoulder Dodo smooths down his
ruffled coat, fixing his beady eyes on Bruno
as if ready to say something.

But no, he shoots down again in three
bounds, runs over to the fireplace and
fills his pouches with wood shavings.

This morning Bruno is making a climbing tree
for Dodo's cage. What a brilliant idea! Dodo
is thrilled and, wide awake, he climbs up it,
jumps about and throws himself from it. What
a pity we have to go to bed. Bruno and Mary wish
they could stay up and watch him
play all night.

Dodo has made a pile of sand in a corner
of his cage. He likes digging holes in
it, rather like Bruno and Mary when they
are at the seaside. Every other day the
children clean out the cage.

Dodo's instinct tells him to hoard
things, so they have to be careful to
clean out the cage thoroughly. When
they have finished, Dodo makes his
nest once more, happy to be clean.

'Come and see my baby hamsters,' Christine says to
her friends one day. Dodo is a male and won't have
any babies. The brother and sister peer into the
cage to look at the new-born babies. Bruno is
really disappointed.
'Aren't they ugly! They're bland and have no fur.'
Mary doesn't agree and finds them really quite
sweet. The babies are tiny and look a little
peculiar. Their eyes and ears are still only
slits, but they can already crawl and wriggle
over to their mother to suckle.
'Don't look too closely,' Christine warns them.
'You will scare their mother. She will think
you are going to take them away from her.'

They place a piece of material
over the cage, so as not to frighten
the mother. Peering through a slit
Christine says: 'The mother drinks
a lot of milk. In a fortnight you
won't recognise these ugly babies
because they will be as handsome as
Dodo. Please come and see them again.'

A fortnight later the baby hamsters look really pretty. Christine puts them in her doll's house to play. They climb around all over the place, exploring and having such fun!

33

It's very odd. Dodo hasn't come out
of his nest this evening.
'Leave him in peace!' says mother.
But Bruno and Mary can't rest
without Dodo.

The next morning there is still no Dodo.
'This time I'm going to have a look,' says
Bruno. He opens the cage and lifts up the
little house. Dodo isn't there! There is
no doubt about that. The hamster has run
away, but how could he have escaped?
No one can make anything of it. Where
could he be? Bruno and Mary are
extremely upset.
'What might he want to eat?' Mother asks
herself. They open the door of the cage
and put a tasty lump of cheese, some
bread, seeds and raisins inside to lure
Dodo back if he is hungry. They call,
'Dodo, Dodo, come along!'

Silence.

Mum looks for Dodo in the cupboards,
Mary looks behind the curtains,
Bruno opens all the wardrobes and
Dad sweeps behind the cooker.

No Dodo!

Mum looks under the mattress, Mary
rummages through the drawers, and
Bruno looks along the shelves,
and Dad behind the mirrors.

No Dodo!

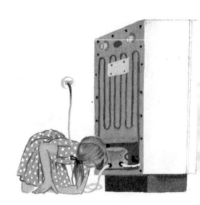

Mum hunts under the beds,
Dad looks under the carpets,
Bruno peers inside the freezer
and Mary checks the fridge.

No Dodo!

Mum pulls back all the cushions,
Dad goes to see the neighbours,
Bruno searches the dustbin and
Mary searches the sewing basket.

No Dodo!

Finally, everyone feels very fed up!

But what is that little noise? Nobody
moves, they all listen ... Yes it is a
tiny rustling sound.
'It's coming from here,' Mum whispers,
pointing to a row of books. Nobody
had thought of looking there. They
clear the books off the shelf and
there, behind the big dictionary,
Dad finds Dodo's new nest.
He is furious.

'Will you please get rid of this
animal. He has gnawed through three
of my books. He is nothing but
trouble. I don't want to see any
more of him!'
'Please Dad, let us keep Dodo. We'll
buy some better books with the money
we have saved. Please Dad, please!'

'I would rather you bought a
lock for that troublemaker's cage!'
Bruno and Mary jump for joy.
'Thank you, Dad, thank you!'

Dodo is hungry and goes back into
his cage to eat a big piece of cheese.
He has already forgotten everything,
but it's the last time he'll go out
on his own. That's for sure!

Chippy,
the Racoon

It is a quiet night and the moon is shining over the
Canadian forest. The woodcutters have been hard at

work all day, but they have shut the doors of their log huts
and now they are fast asleep.

A little white muzzle with a black mask peeps out of a hole in the hollow trunk of the old red maple tree and two beady, bright eyes look out. It looks like a bear cub, but in fact it's Chippy the racoon. He is going to go down to the river to fish for his dinner. Cruncher and Trotter, his two brothers, are still asleep with Mother Racoon. Chippy climbs down the tree very carefully, sticking his claws into the bark, as Mother Racoon does. Then he runs down to the river, just like a little bear. All he can think of are all those fishes he is going to catch for his dinner. Chippy can see very well at night. Better watch out all you little fishes, a hungry racoon is on his way!

But what's this? Someone has got here
before me? Greedy Chippy is taken by
surprise. It's his two cousins who live
by the river, Splasher and Paddler. They
live in a hollow oak on the riverbank.
It's hardly surprising that they should
be the first to gorge themselves on
fresh fish.
'Good fishing, Cousin Chippy!'

Just a flip of his paw and Chippy
has pinched a wriggling little
fish from them. And he has already
gulped down one fish. Flop.
The three racoons glide gracefully
into the middle of the river. The
water is cold, but it is such fun
swimming, fishing and playing
about in the river.

Chippy gets out of the water with a shrimp in each paw. He rinses them in the river, then cracks their shells with his teeth and munches them. He eats everything except the tail and the pincers. His two cousins do the same. The woodcutters will find the leftovers of the meal on the river bank. Meanwhile Mother Racoon slowly ambles down to the river. Cruncher and Trotter follow close behind her.

Each has the same furry ears edged in
white as Chippy, the same black tip of the
nose and white whiskers. But look at their
funny black masks! They are proud of the
dark rings round their tails: these markings
prove that they are no longer
babies. Behind them comes Old
Rocky, their neighbour who
loves catching frogs!

Chippy, Cruncher and Trotter were born in the spring.
They have been able to do things for themselves since
the autumn, but if a wolf or lynx dared to approach
them, Mother Racoon would come to their defence.
With bristling fur, the whole family
would show their teeth and claws! Mother Racoon will
keep an eye on her children for a few more months
yet, until they are almost grown-up.

The river might have been made just for playing
and having fun. The racoons wallow and splash to
their heart's content. Then they chase each other along
the river bank. Whoops! Old Rocky has let
go of a frog. 'Go and play somewhere else and
leave me to fish in peace', he grumbles.
'Quick into the water,' screech the baby racoons.

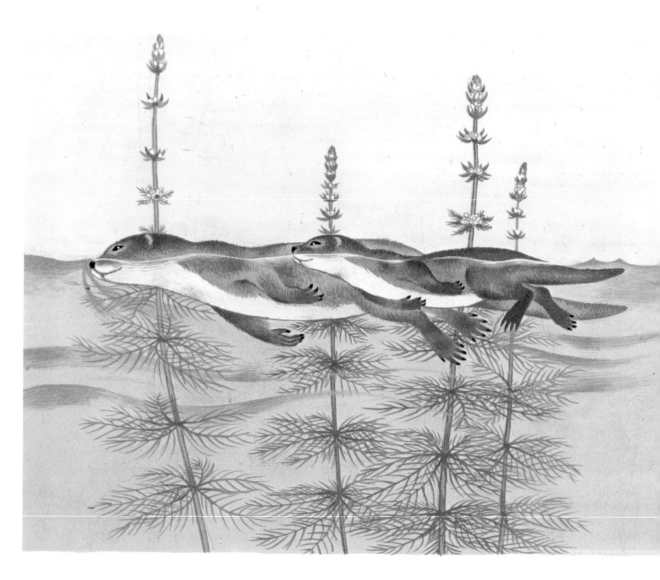

'Beat you to the beaver's lodge!' cries
Paddler, who is practising his swimming
with Cruncher and Trotter.
'Just look at them floundering around,'

says the otter to his cub.
'None of them can swim as well as us.'
They glide swiftly and silently
through the water, overtaking the racoons.

Enough fooling around for now, thinks Chippy,
and he sticks his nose in the air and looks at the
moon. At the same time he rummages around under
the soil, the stones and the moss. He can find
seeds, crunchy insects and juicy little snails
without even looking.

And Chippy is by far
the best when it comes
to climbing trees –
whether galloping up a
trunk or springing
from branch to branch.
It's very handy when
it comes to looking
for tasty birds' eggs.
'You won't find any
at this time of year,'
growls the big black
bear, who has come to
the river for a drink.
The racoons are afraid,
but he soon goes away.

There are plenty of other dangers in the forest and the little racoons always have to be on the look out for any shadow that moves … Chippy, Cruncher and Trotter can tell who this is by his black and white stripy coat. It's the skunk and she could easily spray them with musk. No racoon could possibly go back to his family with that awful smell on his fur. The racoons quickly change direction, taking a safer route.

Chippy comes across his mother munching
mushrooms and gobbling the elderberries.
Between them they will eat the lot!

The night still isn't over and the racoons meet up
at the crooked tree to play at acrobatics. Old
Rocky looks around for a corner in which to sleep.

Cruncher and Paddler aren't at all sleepy and want to
carry on playing. They would like another swim
in the moonlight.

It is getting light and soon it will be day.
Neither the big nor the little racoons waste
a moment of their time. Some continue playing
while the rest either eat more or fall asleep.
Cruncher is perched on a rock and is munching
away at his shrimp. He doesn't know that he is
being watched.

There is no need to be frightened. It is a friend
watching him. Kenny is eight. He is the son of Peter,
the forester who is in charge of replanting the
forest. Kenny feels sad as he watches the racoons
play. He knows that the old red maple tree is going
to be cut down early in the morning. Kenny's father
says that the tree has become dangerous both to
people and to the young trees that have been planted,
and that it has to come down before winter starts.

Kenny wanted to come to work with his father. He
has filled his bag with many different presents
with which to tempt his friends to a new home in
a hollow tree close to the river. Racoons have
lived there before. The lucky things! They will
find a home ready and waiting for them, and in it
will be Kenny's presents: corn, biscuits and even
some honey-flavoured sweets!

Kenny crouches out of sight and watches his friends.
There is a terrible cracking sound, then a thud which
shakes the whole forest. The great red maple has
come down! The little racoons stop their playing
for a moment ...

But the fine weather has come back. Chippy, Cruncher
and Trotter haven't a care in the world and stretch
out in the morning sun for a snooze.

Kenny feels cold in spite of his fur
jacket and heavy boots. But he keeps very
still. All of a sudden a sound makes him
jump and the racoons spring to attention.
Mother Racoon is calling. What is
happening? There is a rustle of movement
and the treading of light feet...

66

It's the fox! Kenny observes the scene
from his hiding place, terrified for the
safety of the racoons. Mother Racoon arches
her back in defence and the little
racoons shout:
'We're not babies any more! We have sharp
claws and we're just as clever as you!'

They huddle together some distance away from the fallen tree. The engines are droning and the saws are whining and the lumberjacks are working busily. With shrill little cries Mother Racoon keeps saying:
'Follow me and keep close together!' Kenny watches them slinking away through the trees.

Look! Chippy is going off on his own ... He climbs up
a tree and clings to one of the branches. He stops,
sniffs the air and then springs to the next tree.
Kenny follows him, without letting him out of his
sight. Chippy nimbly leaps from branch to branch.
But where is he going? Meanwhile Kenny loses
sight of the rest of the family ...

What a funny little thing Chippy is. It's
almost as if he were looking for a shelter
in our house, now his home is gone!

Mmm! What a wonderful smell of toast and bacon.
It's breakfast time.
'I'm hungry,' says Kenny.

Kenny takes care to tread very softly,
even though his heart is beating loudly.
He is still following Chippy, who seems
to have made up his mind to pay his
family a visit. He hasn't come
to rummage through the dustbins,
as so many racoons do. It's a
good thing the dogs aren't
there, or there would be
trouble.

Kenny quietly follows Chippy into the house and
closes the door. Then he slips his hand into
his pocket for a sugar lump and gently holds it
out to the greedy little racoon ... Chippy
refuses it. A sugar lump is too hard and dry
for him! He drinks some of the dog's
water, then dips his sugar lump in it ...
all that's left is a sugary taste
on his paw. Chippy isn't
at all scared of Kenny now.

'If I kept you with me,' Kenny says
to Chippy, 'I could take you back
to the village and put you in our
garden and we could play together.'
But Chippy cries out shrilly,
reminding Kenny that he is a
wild animal and that his
home is in the forest by
the river. He lives at night
and sleeps by day!
Kenny suddenly remembers
the old hollow tree and
the other racoons. He
had almost forgotten
all about it!

He sighs deeply and says:
'Let's go and find your family, little racoon.'
Kenny knew that the racoons would be clever
and greedy enough to find their new home!

And it's there that they will spend the
winter, fast asleep so they won't get cold.
When spring comes Chippy, Cruncher and
Trotter will be grown-up and able to
look after themselves.

Little Owl

Today the carpenter has some work to do in the belfry.
Michael is going along with his father; Sophie is
staying in the garden; and Mum is preparing dinner.

Dad is adjusting the tone
of the bells and Michael is
exploring the belfry.
He clambers down to the
floor, holding the beams
tightly so as not to fall.
Suddenly he hears a strange
noise:
'Twit, twoo . . .!'
'Come here Dad quickly!
Which little animal is making
that noise?'

Dad comes up to have a look.
'It's a baby owl. Poor little thing has probably lost
its parents. I expect it's hungry.'
The lonely little owl whimpers as if to say yes.

'Yes you're hungry little owl,' says Michael. He holds out his hand, but the little owl sits down and leans back, displaying her long claws in angry defence.

Michael tries to slip his hand behind her, but the owl is too sharp to be cheated and quickly nips his finger.

'Ouch, that hurts. Let go!' But the little owl doesn't let go. So Michael slips his other hand behind her and holds her wings back.

'I'll just have to take you with me, seeing that you are holding on so tightly, you rascal!'

86

Sophie is thrilled with
the surprise that Michael
brings. By now the little
owl has let go of the
boy's hand. She sits on the
table and stares up at
Sophie. Then she quietly
coos: 'Twoo Twoo.'

'See, she already likes me,' says Sophie, stroking
her. 'Aren't her feathers soft and fluffy!' Michael is
pleased that he knows what type of bird he has found.
'She's a little owl,' he explains, 'and very hungry.
Let's feed her Sophie! You go and see what Mum has
in the fridge and I'll stay here and look after her.'

Sophie brings some
pieces of liver; Little
Owl swallows them whole.
Now she has food inside
her she feels sleepy.

'Let's put her in the attic so she can sleep
peacefully.' Sophie fetches some old rags, but Little
Owl only huddles up next to them. Owls don't make
nests, so they don't need anything to sleep on.

Sophie decides to take Little Owl to school in a basket.
The teacher puts her on top of a pile of books for
everybody to see.
'Her claws are even longer than my cat's,'
says Sophie.
'She will use them for hunting,' says the teacher.
'She will start flying and will go off in search of
food in the evenings: mice, slugs and little insects.'

When gardeners and farmers
hear her hooting they will
say: 'That is our friend
the owl; she protects our
vegetables and wheat. No-
one must ever hunt her.'
'Where are her ears?'
asks one of the children.
'Hidden amongst her
feathers. Little Owl can
hear and see much better
than us. Her vision is
exceptionally good.'

Little Owl listens to the
teacher. She suddenly
straightens herself up
and makes a little bow.
The children laugh in
surprise. Then she swivels
her head right round
and looks behind her.

Sophie gives her a piece of meat and puts her back
in the basket so she can take her home.

Little Owl is tame now and
will eat from people's hands.
At night time she walks up
and down the attic cooing
softly to herself.
Yesterday the attic was full
of down because Little Owl
is moulting. Her new feathers
and grey with white flecks
and her tail has dark stripes.
Her face is still pale and
her eyes and beak are a pretty
yellow.

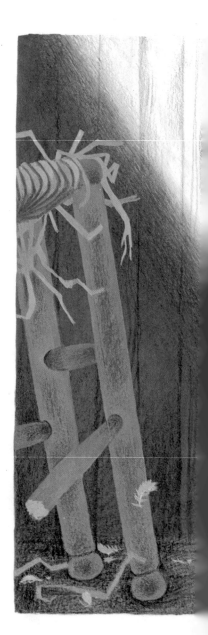

In the evening she sits on
the attic windowsill and
chatters to Michael as he
waters the garden.
'Twit Twoo, twit twoo,'
are the only sounds she
can make. Michael answers
her calls and sprays her
with a few drops of water.
Little Owl likes her shower.
She puffs out her feathers
and carefully preens herself.

97

Little Owl is gradually growing up. Her wings are
stronger and her feathers are growing. This evening
Sophie and Michael go down to taste the redcurrants.
In the twilight and high up in the sky the swallows
call to one another as they search for insects.
Sophie spots a bat and they watch its crooked flight.
To the children's amazement Little Owl silently
takes off, flying high into the sky.

She crosses the garden to the poplar trees on the
edge of the meadow.
'Let's follow her!' says Michael.
'Twit twoo, twit twoo!' calls Little Owl.
'I would rather not', replied Sophie, frightened.
'Oh come on, there's no danger, it's our little
friend calling us.' Sophie and Michael run towards
the meadow which is covered in dew.

The night-time flowers open and fill the air with exotic scent.

'Twit twoo, twit twoo', calls Little Owl as she flies round the field.

'Tyook tyook!'

The reed-like call is the toad answering Little Owl. He is telling her that the moon is rising amongst the clouds.

Not everything sleeps at
night. There is a little
light shining in the hedge:
it is a glow-worm. Michael
picks it up and holds it
in the palm of his small
hand. It has a round
shiny belly.
'Twit twoo, twit twoo.'
Little Owl is hunting.
Suddenly all the creatures
go quiet. Then the night-
time noises start up again.
A rabbit crosses the
meadow and a nightingale
sings a few clear notes.

A clumsy butterfly brushes against Sophie's cheek and falls to the ground. 'Don't touch its wings or it won't be able to fly any more,' says Michael. He slips a twig under the butterfly and it clings to it.

'Oooh!' cries Sophie. 'It has a face like Little Owl!' It's true. The moth's wings have a pattern on them which looks like an owl's face. Sophie and Michael come back through the vegetable garden. The timid toad is hiding behind a stone but a hedgehog is shuffling along the path. He is looking for his supper!

Tonight Sophie and Michael will sleep with their
window wide open so they can listen to Little
Owl and the nightingale until they fall asleep.

Little Owl doesn't come home until much later. From now on she will find her own food. She hunts for little creatures such as caterpillars, beetles and lizards.

One morning she doesn't come back. She has chosen a new home in a tall poplar tree. Sophie finds Little Owl asleep on a branch, far out of reach.

Autumn comes.
Every evening when it is
fine Sophie and Michael run
down to the meadow to see
their nocturnal friends.
They find all sorts of new
things: lovely fat
mushrooms, a family of
dormice, snails . . .

Little Owl often comes
to see her friends.
They call her by
copying her cry:
'Twit twoo, twit twoo.'
She lands on Sophie's
clenched fist, bends
her head and looks at
her. She always looks
so wise!

There is a lot of noise this evening. Little Owl is
calling and someone is answering her. They sound
like cats miaowing. Little Owl has found a boyfriend.
You can clearly see two birds perched next to each
other. Now they are cooing to one another and
rubbing each other's beaks.

They move into a hole in the poplar tree and Little
Owl lays three round, speckled eggs. She will sit on them
for four weeks. Her mate feeds her in silence. Neither of
the two birds makes a sound during all this time. They
don't want anyone to find their precious eggs.

Then one evening Sophie finds bits of egg shell at
the foot of the tree. Little Owl's babies have
been born. Dad says that baby owls are very tough.
There is no cosy nest for them and no one feeds
them. They don't eat anything the day they are born. The
next day they eat the food their parents
put down before them all by themselves.

A month later they go out hunting with their parents.
Before long there won't be enough insects in the

meadow to feed the whole of the family. The little
owls will have to travel further in search of food.

The young female owl moves into the belfry where Little Owl was born, the second baby makes its home in a willow tree and the youngest one goes into the forest.

Winter and summer alike Little Owl will spend the rest of her long life in the meadow with the same mate.